Coastal Wonder

Coastal Wonder

Poems

James Leggett

*"Individually, we are one drop.
Together, we are an ocean."*

\-   Ryunosuke Satoro

Contents

III.

IV.

V.

Coastal Wonder

I.

Oceanfront

I stare at a blue planet
its waves interrogating the shore
while withholding all of its secrets
I feel that primal urge to rush in
fully aware I am out of my element
the dangerous method of tide and current
tension rising into its natural crescendo

the horizon could be worlds away
and hazy sunlight ignites the surface
above the parade of fish and their stories
the water is colder than it would seem
a small shock to the touch of flesh
recognizing the hold of its power
an entirety filled with potential

I only drift into this kingdom briefly
swimming and sinking and floating by
the coast an assembly of sandy shores
summer has a way of flourishing
allowing land and sea to intertwine
there's magic to the way the sun sets beneath it
surrendering itself to all of this wonder

Back Alley

outside my apartment is the uproar
of alley cats shouting at the night sky

their cries are comically loud like
they just stepped out of an MGM cartoon

but the cries are also real
the hunger in their mouths not an act

as they fight and feed on any scraps
they find in overheated garbage cans

spilled over the hot pool of summer
evenings when temperatures refuse to drop

and it's a tough look to be so hungry and angry
sorry - "hangry"
enough that you'll let your worst screams

push back against your competition
looking for the same meal as you

for if you continue unfed then
who knows what comes out of

desperate mouths with only the desire
to survive another night

Assurance of Pardon

she tells me it's my mother's eyes
and my father's everything else

as I stand up, holding a hymnal with two hands
they notice what a fine young man I've become

at my age my father held a daughter
and signed divorce papers

she's not sure if she has one year left or several
you could say the same about all of us

I've been asked if I'll be a pastor too one day
I say I like poetry if that counts for anything

the daily devotions tell you friendship is special
and love saves everyone if you let it

they prefer sermons that don't get political
cause no one comes to church for that

all are welcomed but none are invited
if you don't see yourself in the statement

"Go to Hell" has a lot more weight to it
when it's ordered by holy men in holy power

the future looks weak and attendance is low
with my demographic

we sing about mercy and keep tongues
held exactly where they belong

God forgives so you don't need to
bloodshed on dollar bills is nothing but the blood

sins of the father passed down gracefully
screams of the helpless mistaken for worship

Cool

Steve McQueen rips out dialogue from scripts
and we understand what it means to be cool
his registry untethered by verbal response

blonde hair, crease for a mouth
tongue forced out of monologue
emoting through a stare

only the person who turns a scream into a fist
will run mouths into the ground first
before second thoughts begin to ascend

the angry microphone wakes itself
takes context to elevate its fiction
delivers lines as weaponized persuasion

it's one thing to fear a villain
and another to know what they're capable of
given the right circumstances

if acting is reacting then how do you react
to what forms in closed mouths, nervously ready
to part lips like a red sea?

if only the outcry that arrives instinctively
ever floated the idea of Steve McQueen
saying all that can be said after the words
have been ripped out of the page

Fire Weather

there's a red flag warning in Central Pennsylvania
as we drive out of one of those mid-June
thunderstorms that rains
relentlessly with a vendetta
before transitioning back to blue skies
as if nothing happened at all
any real danger exists wherever it may
though the orange sun above
shows it has real staying power
the car's air-conditioner works overtime
while we discuss the rise of AI and
how eras don't always know their ending
out there workers are still on strike
and the fire warning is in effect until 8pm
with any new beginning we naturally try our best
to hold onto some semblance of what was
today's Microsoft Outlook outage was temporary
but long enough to convince us we're off the grid

Discipline

I wait my turn in the one-lane
traffic circle where restless vehicles
are fueled by impulses to drive anywhere
and get there quickly

it's the season when pollen
infiltrates my lungs
as practice of ritual
and I can't always speak

car horns are accompanied by
cursing that rolls off anonymous tongues
and it must be a kind of discipline
to sit and wait
told "no" when you only respond to yes
patience as a virtue
while time waits for no one

to be forced to stay in your lane
even when there's only one and
we're all here together
living out this communal experience
where hands collectively reach above
searching for any assurance

it's a lineup of cars now, all stubbornly ready
to escape this moment like a bad dream
that ends when you abruptly rush back to life

to excuse oneself from this type of behavior
as if you never intended to be here
chasing away while eyes see the machine
and know the cog for all its worth

Bloodsoaked

I step out of my building and into an ongoing
debate between one of my neighbors and our
super. He's complaining about the front door and
how warped it's gotten, to the point that our
bronze keys barely work and it feels like we're
trapped outside of our homes. Before I can walk
past, the neighbor motions to me, calls me buddy
which he often does, and asks for me to weigh in.
I usually avoid confrontation because I never
have the words in front of me, or the fight to
back them up. And the super whips back, says
only his father can talk to him this way. And it's
already the heat in the morning, that thick layer
that adds enough tension while sweat blares out
all over the conflict. I have to imagine this is
about more than just a door and when the air is
this heavy and cruel perhaps we all bring out the
worst parts of ourselves. Blades drawn and
hungry for battle. I offer a shrug cause I don't
know what else to do, not that I disagree about
the warped door but my Via ride is far enough
away to not know any of this and is about to
leave. I can already feel the neighbor being let
down, my inability to choose a side is its own
admission of defeat. And the nickname "buddy"
becomes a betrayal in its own right. If the stakes

are this high already I can't imagine how the rest of the day goes, when the heat is all that is likely to remain. Maybe words are more bark than bite and maybe a knife has no choice but to draw blood when it cuts deep enough.

II.

Free Will

Free will has a nice ring even with a price tag
attached to it. There's no longer smoke hanging
above Manhattan but plagues feel plausible
sometimes. The ones we're aware of at least,
every frog and lotus sent to shake things up a bit.
At least we can still discover viruses to take our
breaths away. Dread is the second you arrive at
gunpoint with nothing but your freedom. Making
a choice means there's every option we didn't
pick and it's been years since we spoke. If it's
failure on us to keep in touch then at least
there's nostalgia to recreate ourselves.
Sometimes it feels like life is one misstep away
from gravity taking over. We can't choose when
we leave the womb and enter this world but the
title on our LinkedIn profiles feels earned. Fear
and hatred have already figured out how to
coexist. It's easy to say there's no place like home
as soon as there's nowhere to run. Glory
Hallelujah can be found on tongues already living
in the ground. Before we inhale the dust and ash,
let's watch as instinct moves closer to insanity.

Quality Control

it's another day where every street corner
is baptized in sweat and rain
and cloud-heavy skies watch and give approval

the start and stop of downpour creates
a rhythm to the afternoon and I mistake
the floor for comfort
coughing for a living
with steps that don't understand lineage

I was shy once and can still look like the boy
who sits in the backseat and quietly accepts
that worlds pass by with enough time

light pours through pleated curtains
begging for forgiveness
for always leaving

my lungs feel like expiration
as breathable air becomes smoke
and the currency of a single breath
feels dangerously out of reach

enough with the agony
that only lives to die
let maternal hands cradle heads
into crowns of relief

we can thank each and every sunrise
for showing us what it looks like
to begin again

Heavy is the Crown

heavy is the crown you've inherited
through righteous rites of passage
that dripped poison through ceremony
a masterclass of vocal exchange
poise your throne and install your legacy
with no need for repercussion

when hands darker than yours
cover their heads in terror
you cover yours with fine jewels
as your proud parents hold back tears
you've become the person they've always
wanted you to be
free to navigate this life as you see fit

Decision to Stay

I sign the lease to begin the second year of what
my previous landlord calls "independent living." If
I'm alone in my apartment speaking it becomes
the poetry itself with the courage to listen. It's
air-conditioning season. My window faces east
so I don't feel the afternoon sun that reminds me
what summer is capable of. There are kids on the
other side of the alley who jump on trampolines
and howl with the unflinching joy of
adolescence. And I smile and shrug at the same
time because I was there once and can never go
back. Not the same way but each of us contains a
small young voice rattling in the cage when
adulting becomes less appealing the more we
accept it. I no longer wait for storms to show
rainbows but rather enjoy the downpour as
revenge for the oppressive heat. If we ever feel
lonely then it's crowded rooms who have bad
timing. When I say I'm nervous about the future I
mean I feel the weight of things that haven't
happened yet. I can lie on this floor and admit
my heart is full and still screams with hunger.

Ferdinand

My grandfather was named Ferdinand and read me the story of Ferdinand the Bull anytime I stayed over. A bull that was built like steel and filled to the brim with raw power. A machine of violence to be the main attraction in Madrid. But the bull chose smelling flowers over fighting. I don't remember the pictures but I remember the way my grandfather turned the pages. The artist that he was, with a special connection to paper. He understood the way a hand can unite with a page to create wonder. All while the bull lived in grassy sunkissed plains to inhale the floral breeze. To be the size of a fighter and turn your passion to beauty over bloodsport. Trading in hooves for gentle tools, undefined by combat. The bull chose another life for itself. My grandfather's hands were the tools that could drum and paint and turn watercolors into scenery. The hand as a guidance, taking brushstrokes across a canvas and creating natural worlds. These are the only two Ferdinand's I've ever known and I met them both in the same house.

boygenius, Live in Toronto

it's officially the longest day of the year and
my flight was one hour and one country away

it's been four years since I've seen my nephews
and they embrace me like a prodigal son learning
the language of home

my sister rises in motherhood and wears
punk rock energy
as we gather outside Budweiser Stage for the
show to start

the band goes on at 9:30 or maybe 9:45
which is daytime even as the sun burns
itself alive

the kids wear neckties and tattoos with their
pent up desire to turn the sky upside down
and call it a dancefloor

as the moon collapses into its waxing crescent
and we are blades of grass in the tune of summer

the boys are back in town and tonight
we are all boys
with the screams of unified youth
who speak in lyrics

and rebel against the tyranny of old fathers
who breathe lessons instead of music

in a blink it's Phoebe & Lucy & Julien
rock gods taking the stage with their
electric weapons

everyone shouts and loses their minds
to drown out the idea that this place
was once a graveyard

silently abrupted by vacancy
stripped summer of all its unfiltered magic

starting tomorrow the days will feel shorter
but music refuses to die or ever stay dead

for tonight we'll raise guitars and crushed cans
and sing with voices that ride off into the sunset

Out of the Comfort

in the calendar year that starts
and ends in the halls of winter
I promised I wouldn't leave dishes
in the sink long enough
to overwhelm the kitchen
and learn to cook
out of a necessity
that's defined by
more than just hunger
I only figured out how to read
the sky in reflections
of wet puddles
drowning blue sneakers alive
while heads stay down
I want to dance
in the melancholy of a song
softly sung but with volume
to distract from the fear
of what happens
when dusk rises above
blackout curtains
and mouths lose the
desire to speak
as if speech no longer
carries any warmth
and silence takes on new

meaning when we've lived
in the night too long
the walls of a room
are nothing but walls after
every one of us leaves

III.

Jukebox

patiently or not I wait for the chorus
the repetition to revitalize itself
the jukebox is an old tired thing
filled with quarters and throwbacks
living at the edge of the bar
drowned out by the cacophony
of conversations rising and falling
with drunken slurs and closing out tabs
circling the drain of half finished whiskeys
soon they will leave and look out at the moon
and serenade it to stay a little longer
to keep the music alive before we push
more of ourselves into the past
growing but not always gaining
they wonder why we're not seen
dancing on the roof
wandering into a lullaby
that lives inside the same mouths
unable to articulate what happened
whatever song was on the jukebox
has already ended and I didn't
remember the chorus in time
to hum along with the journey home
I venture outside where the heat is like
a second door you can't help but stand in
"Hot as Hell out there!" I hear from behind me

a cry loud enough and with a clarity
that knows what surrender feels like

The Devils' Home Game

a clash of blades
fury of sticks fighting to survive
chasing a puck in every direction
stationary cries from a lively crowd
summon purpose from potential

in any second the skates screech
across the ice in drive and thunder
speeding towards the goal line
the puck a blip in constant motion

where bodies break and collide
their violence birthed in method
channeling primal rage
to find some kind of victory

sticks rise and then fall
propelling the puck into eternity
the hit of the net unleashes
a crowd's deafening chant
"Howl" begins to play

South Korean Revenge Films

I love American revenge movies, every John Wick
and Mandy who let us get our kicks watching
violence and rooting for their bloodlust. Cause
what kind of monster kills dogs and unified
fronts let us champion good guys taking out
objectively bad men. But I get even more out of
South Korean revenge because those films, every
Oldboy or I Saw the Devil, give no pretense to
vengeance. There's no justice in the hammer
crunching a skull and the quest is no hero's
journey. Revenge is a ghost with nothing left to
do but haunt the souls who took everything that
gave life purpose. And their deaths, whether or
not justified, can't raise the living back. We're
satisfied watching dirtbags get theirs, but when
do we stop cheering and realize the dish served
cold can't feed the hunger that fights to death
but doesn't know how to die?

Late Night

My Uber driver picks me up in his white Honda
Accord sometime after two in the morning.
Emphasis on sometime as the minutes have
given themselves over to this era of night. I'm a
version of myself excused from the thought
process of daytime but fueled by the
consciousness that can't succumb to sleep. I
rarely find myself up at this hour, except when
cold sweat unites the sheets to my body. And my
eyes open not to morning light but to the same
pitch black I originally closed them to. When the
preacher closes the book from Friday to Sunday
we see only the gravity of the situation. Even
knowing there will eventually be light we're still
meant to live in the darkness for a while. Time is
no longer the light on my phone or the
expectation of dawn. The driver and I agree on
silence while I watch Newark turn into Jersey
City. Each random streetlight is as lonely as the
select few who've chosen to stay up this late.
Roaming the streets like echoes of the previous
day, marching from bars and airports to
wherever will invite them next. Yesterday falls
into the past tense while memory bleeds into the
place of dreaming. The promise of light and fear

of dark are only a matter of how willing the eyes
are to stay open.

Coastal Flood Advisory

I'm able to get to the food market just in time
before closing. They're calling it early due to the
impending storm and I exchange the tap of a
card for small necessities: a carton of milk, a
bottle of vitamin water, a dozen large eggs. The
forecast says rain will start anytime now, and
maybe it has and I simply haven't noticed. Maybe
I've stood in enough storms to never recognize
being drenched. I wonder what would happen if I
developed gills to breathe underwater, like the
Creature from the Black Lagoon. To live under
the surface and only rise up when desire enters
the swampy lagoon terrain. Like a lot of classic
monsters, the Creature's biggest crime was being
misunderstood. And violence still leads to an
outcome depending on which side of the barrel
you stand on. And before I can ruminate on this
any further, the cashier points to the door, an
insurmountable rush of gray skies on the other
side. It looks and feels like the beginning of any
disaster movie, when people run from
abandoned cars as if the sky itself is chasing
them. And I look down at the items I've
purchased, as if this will help me from whatever
apocalypse should arrive today. It feels like some
bad omen existing between coincidental and

inevitable. Like being in a dream where everything is off but you don't stop and think to ask why. The cashier apologizes but insists they have to close, and I understand and move out to where others are racing to their homes. Each of us our own candle in the wind, standing in the great approach, holding close to that which flickers in the dark.

Pine Grove Mills, PA

We walk out of Pine Grove Hall with the buzz of a
few beers and the lull of a sleepy town which
knows its curfew has already begun. The night is
quiet, almost too quiet for me and it's been ten
years since we graduated. It's kind of funny how
time tricks you into thinking there's always more
to come. Before we dive straight into all the
places we've been to, let's admit there's
simplicity that isn't easy to replicate. And not
sure if it's wisdom or just understanding that
certain things slip away when hands forget what
they were holding onto in the first place.

I can thank remote working and staying in touch
cause half of those names are now just that,
names, faces that existed once upon a time. I was
always bad with names especially when the
school year began. We can treat ourselves
to old glory while the bar closes early and we
move towards the night's end. The symphony of
drunken laughter that would greet any Saturday
night has removed itself and we've learned to
accept parting ways as a form of travel. The
home away from home is temporary even if it
wants to be timeless. The clock on the kitchen

wall has several ways of telling the exact same story.

Intelligent Design

My father says suffering is a part of the human experience and most of us aren't qualified to handle it. Our education includes algebra and literary classics but not what happens when a loved one dies fighting an illness they never asked for. The cycle breaks when the parent puts the child to rest and not the other way around. Sunday school helps with spiritual walks until you arrive in the hands of leaders who like control. When we dig into the ground and bury our own does God think we're renovating his house? My dad's final sermon was on zoom and we've seen better finales than that. I'm told I need a group of like minded young people to grow in faith and call abuse "not my problem." Love is kind when it isn't cruel. Logan Roy dies and the kids are still fucked from the start. Every man will become his own tragedy instead of going to therapy. Everyone pretends the pandemic never happened, even the ones still wearing masks. The same children who frown may not know what it actually means to smile. We can look up at the same sky and come to our own conclusions. I can drive through a white orbit of snow, where all I see are tailights and think they were angels sent from above.

IV.

Tears of a Mother

the stream of water falls off the roof
to create a wall of flooding

and our plans to go to the beach are stalled
long enough for us to take it personally

cause what is vacation if not
a moment of time never meant to last

it feels tough to surrender yourself to summer
while Mother Nature weeps across the ocean

those getting out of the water simply
feel the continuous weight of being soaked

rinsed in the seaweed and salt like the ocean
violently rejected them back

and the parental figure mourns
for every child that ever was or will be

the world has a few billion years on us while
we can't see the radar to contextualize the blip

the news station in the living room mentions
it being the hottest day on record in the Midwest

and the season is far from over, as time
drifts further with the hammering of raindrops

on every surface of the planet, creating waves
to rush over its own madness

Unison Reading

we're gonna need a bigger boat
or a bigger God

the word is made flesh and the tongue
has a careful way of learning

if we're all placing bets let's unite
in more ways than just how we grieve

I've recited prayers enough
that the words remember me instead

winter occupies space and still promises
to return after the world blooms

not everything has to be about you
or rather you & me

okay make it us
and if we sing let's sing with intent

in our song and blood in the cup
for those seeking refuge

outside of this we all fear life just enough
to tighten our hands into formal amens

old problems breed new leaders
who sharpen teeth with historical text

we can agree to disagree but first let
hands collect any offerings in the plate

and eyes close to the same open sky
that has outlived all of us

Woodland

my parents' backyard is a green country
living in the promise of the sun

where deer silently appear
statues of oakwood silhouette

the nieces and nephew race to the window
to get a glimpse of the wilderness

where the woodland meets the border of Rt. 46
and the deer eat leaves and find shade

each hoof caressing the twigs and grass
surrounded by every decision we've made

the highway is nothing but a hum
a sort of white noise to make you forget

all the ways we took over
building towns and community

shopping malls and diners where kids
hang away from busy adults

even my hometown of Montclair
carries "mount" in the name

for all the bombast of suburban life
and downtown art and culture

there's still the part of nature
embedded in the infrastructure

where the sunlight grows
and deer gallop and stride

with the confidence of knowing
how to call a place your own

Doctrine

The tone is in need of repair
a remake of threadbare sounds
reaching into my lungs
to take out a confession.

My prayers have become relics
old archival musings
vague enough to be heard
by no God who listens.

I've never sat in the booth that requires
sin in exchange for mercy
blood spilled out of words into hands
that knows the same sin will
eventually cry for the same mercy.

See the way the tongue moves
the contortion of misused lips
unready for language.

Allow my daily cost to prolong
the agonized rush of routine
standing in open water as waves
push against exposed skin
able to drift without notice.

O father, o fathers
see how the son only returns
after the sin has completed.

Watch as the desire to live
searches for any water
to nourish or rinse away
the same filth resembling flesh.

$10

The sign next to the cash register says
"Contactless" loud enough
to make the $10 bill in my wallet feel worthless.

Like the currency was wiped away and now
it's just crumpled paper in faded brown leather.

$10 used to be the weekly allowance which
allowed me to go to the movies
and get a slice of pizza.

I usually keep at least that much on me as a
safety net when the credit card is declined
or the cashier

insists on being cash only. Except now it's
contactless.
If we learned anything from the pandemic it's all
the ways

we can distance ourselves. How a hand can
distance itself from
the value of money, long enough to see poverty
inside of your palms.

How a door can be both an entrance and an exit
depending on how far away you stand.

There are lines on my face signifying
both the age I am and all the ages I'll never
be again.

I want a new kind of summer.
I've lived in the rain long enough for it
to grow teeth.

I'm close enough to the future to be afraid of it.
I'm neither here nor there, or so I tell myself.

As if they are two sides of the same coin.
Not that that counts for much ever since we lost
contact.

Undercurrent

if only I could pretend
the same strength used to climb mountains
could take me on a pilgrimage
where I arrive with fallen knees to the ground
to simply say, "this is all I've got"

where a breathless amen could travel
across planets to satisfy a judgment
live in fear or rest in peace
the walk to begin again sheds past lives

I block out the night with curtains
and unspoken words
allow thoughts to rhythmically align with prose
my head can lower into the same depths
as the ocean brought to life by lighthouses
so if I should drown I can still see the light
flickering throughout a ravenous sky

the body is its own planet earth with
water rushing throughout in attempts
to save us from self-made destruction
while parched lips sing for thirst to nourish

weakness can be a refuge
from weight stubbornly carried above
standing still is a compromised game
against the will to move
the road ends along with the body
the waters rage through tumultuous storms

Peace in the Valley

I don't mean to sound so morbid discussing
mortality but there is a feeling that every time a
part of us heals, it's a small victory, a lower case
w since the game ends the same for all of us. If
there really is something after this life, it may
simply come down to which god you're praying
to and how often you plead guilty for a lifetime's
worth of sin. I can't imagine a fear of death
outweighing a fear of life. The worries of endless
overdue bills and living through transactions in
order to keep living. Or the mental wellbeing
that isn't so well when the day wears apathy over
its cruel shoulders. Fear not except there's
plenty to be afraid of. Like how time keeps going
even when your balance is shaken, when uneven
concrete presses against the heels of gray Vans.
Maybe now's the time to get into the "what if" of
it all. Our relationship to our past selves and the
way regret reconfigures our memories. How we
strive to learn from our choices and still shudder
at the future. And then there's worry at a
granular level: climate change, political outrage,
past crimes inherited from forefathers. I was
taught to go and sin no more so what excuse is
there now? The bread of life is nourishing and
yet we still keep survival close. We're still

desperate enough to become primal when the world deals an unexpected hand. We're in these mortal bodies one time and we're still trying to make it count. How bones break and skin bleeds and it's all our own. How vulnerable the flesh becomes as it ages, moving further and further away from control. If I find myself standing in the valley, the green pastures with waters and slivers of sun, I pray it's as peaceful as a song. One whose lyrical comfort guides through the end of a breath.

V.

Riptide

I swim carelessly into the riptide
ignited by unsuspecting alarm

pushed into the rage of current
under a sky of sunshine

it's amazing how the skills to swim
become useless in the laws of nature

the wild animal of surf
close enough to steal you away

arms and legs thrashing
panicked into newfound fear

it's easy to feel small in the ocean
and then smaller on the earth

the body naturally desires water
even the water that wrestles you

how I learned to breathe
through desperately holding a breath

how skin that turns red
burns unforgiven in the summer heat

we exist somewhere between sea and space
to behold each world separately

time seemingly minor to their vastness
unassumed by aging the way we are

I only forget how to sink
as soon as I can breathe again

to leave the jungle of ocean
and still yearn for it

we find enough curiosity
in the heart of danger

how a scream for mercy arrives
even when it's undeserved

like looking up at the sun
and seeing nothing but fire

Wild

squinting pale eye
looking for fireflies for attraction
and soft light
the allure of summer dissolves
with mosquitos and gnats
charging through the air
I lit a candle outside
to exist in the backyard evening
filled with glimpses of wildlife
the occasional fox or limping raccoon
who see me as an extension of the outdoors
another being whose existence
breathes in their territory
living on the man made wood clearly marked
away from the natural land
it was years ago that I discovered how my street
ends and becomes a town with green lamp posts
and it was years after that we had that nor'easter
where the giant branch fell onto the street
and no cars could come or go for days
when the sky was so white we could lament
the loss of sunsets and all it entails
only my feet could discover uneven pavement
and how gravity informs each step
though the fallen branch was big enough
to be a line never crossed

Eleventh Hour

the animals march
two by two onto
the boat
a symbol of unity
and the desperation of
two beings
staring into the same abyss
the Ark a big wooden might
able to weather the blackened skies
with anger in their winds

the textbook taught me to raise hands
the gospel taught me to keep them raised
not called on but called
extension to a reachable light
sight unseen
belief in the ether

one hand greets as
the other stays behind
stationary while the former
becomes dominant

a discovery of words
navigator of touch and feel
instrumental in the art of senses

hands on a clock
move succinctly in unison
to create time

a perfect synergy
one and one both at work
while a grandfather
broadcasts the hour
and the Ark stays afloat

but what is a tool's purpose
when it's not in use
who then does it get to serve?

Wreckage Over Worship

Fire ascending from the basement
as the office floorboard caved in
to infiltrate the sanctuary.
A place of worship now a warzone
of missing casualties and shattered faith.
Shattered like stained glass windows
erupting wild smoke into the sky.
How the pulpit which spoke good news
drops into black wreckage.
Enough time for a community to bear witness
and fall to the knees
not in prayer, but a new disbelief.
How I learned to see Cambridge Street
through the absence of a ceiling.
How I now identify a place I grew up
in the flames that consumed it.
If there's any poetry to be found in this
it's the union of broken people
who learned to mourn in these same walls
through funerals and walks of life.
Now find an array of grievances
situated away from the holy ground
guarded for safety as
firefighters confront catastrophe.
When you remove the home from hometown
it's a place you recognize less of

seeing yourself on the outskirts
watching, waiting
unsure of what comes next.

.

Prehistoric

if only each and every dinosaur
who saw the meteor and understood
what it truly means to end
could see us for what we are
not through the lens of
natural history museums
or Spielberg blockbusters
but sharing the same world

as soon as we bit into the fruit
did every war to come find its origin
and root itself in our shame?
we don't fear the meteor as much as ourselves
history is doomed to repeat until
the pages catch fire

Mother Earth cries herself to sleep
watching children breathe in chaos
their charcoaled lips turned to ash
it was us that knocked her up this time

the night sky reveals outer space
as its own kind of eternity
our feet planted on the ground, as gravity tells
us no when our impulse is to fly

nowadays homes sell better as plots of land
reducing what once was to its core
territory makes way to futures
we put a price on a world that brought us life
as we slowly look at fossils
and stare until they become mirrors

Shoreline

let it be simple as the waves
rolling into sandbars
claps of gentle fortitude
lulls of coastal wonder
salt air intoxicating high tide
a quick glimpse into another world
abundance of blue scenery
new eras of August
burnt lips into a smile
crescent moon sailing
adjacent to daybreak
oceanic as a constant
how repetition calms and soothes
relieving sunbathed skin
let it be easy on the touch
sand defined in footprints
the call of the water
the innermost summer
echoed in the breeze

Real Love

I've been taught that there are many different
kinds of love. Familial love, romantic love, God's
love. A big word filled with one syllable across
four letters. Love makes sense on paper but then
again so does tragedy. Like when life doesn't go
according to plan and we step out of the fire,
ashes in the sole of our shoes. I've seen the
sunrise at the top of a mountain and found new
ways to fear falling. Life can feel like an
endurance test with the amount of weight
thrown on our backs, each new burden piling on
top of the last. It feels less a question of if but
when. When the legs beneath us give out and we
come crashing down, each weight falling one
after another. Till we're buried under the rubble
of our own making. All I know is I want a real
love. A real, real love. Like a rescue that arrives
before we get the chance to crumble. The idea
that a burden can be carried by more than just
you. If legs can bend and break then they can
also move. Forward or backward. Misery is a
promise and mercy is a future. I watched a
mother get introduced to her newborn and we
called it love. Loving someone from day one for
simply being here. I saw a loved one till the end
and they were still loved after that. Even in the

rot of a ruined sanctuary, I saw healing in how communal love blossoms. How two hands can hold and find beauty from one palm to another. The heart is a powerful thing. Taking bruises and breaking wide open and still beating. Blood flowing to invigorate and inspire. I want to walk to the edge and never cross it. I want to feel the weight on my shoulders and know I can still breathe. I want music to live in every sunrise I witness. I want tomorrow to arrive without a warning. I want to admit that hate is strong and love is stronger. By the time I get to the end of life, I want to be surprised. Not just for what comes next or how I got there, but by seeing how far love can travel. A real love.

Acknowledgments

To my family and friends. The ones I see regularly, semi-regularly or whenever our paths cross. Please know I would not be here without your love and support.

Made in United States
Orlando, FL
23 January 2024

42838254R00046